12

Something for Nothing

For Mom and Grandma Ida
—A.R.S.

For Charles S. Cohen
—J.M.C.

Clarion Books
a Houghton Mifflin Company imprint
215 Park Avenue South, New York, NY 10003
Text copyright © 2003 by Ann Redisch Stampler
Illustrations copyright © 2003 by Jacqueline M. Cohen
The illustrations were executed in watercolor.
The text was set in 16-point Boton.

www.houghtonmifflinbooks.com

Printed in Singapore

Library of Congress Cataloging-in-Publication Data
Stampler, Ann Redisch.
Something for nothing / by Ann Redisch Stampler ;
illustrated by Jacqueline M. Cohen. • p. cm. • Summary:
In this variation on a Jewish folktale, a dog moves to the
country in search of peace and quiet only to be plagued
by three rowdy cats, but he devises a clever plan to end
their nightly noise. • ISBN 0-618-15982-7 (alk. paper)
[1. Jews—Folklore. 2. Folklore.] I. Cohen, Jacqueline M.
II. Title. • PZ8.1.S7865 So 2003 • 398.2'089'0924—dc21
2002007943

TWP   10 9 8 7 6 5 4 3 2 1

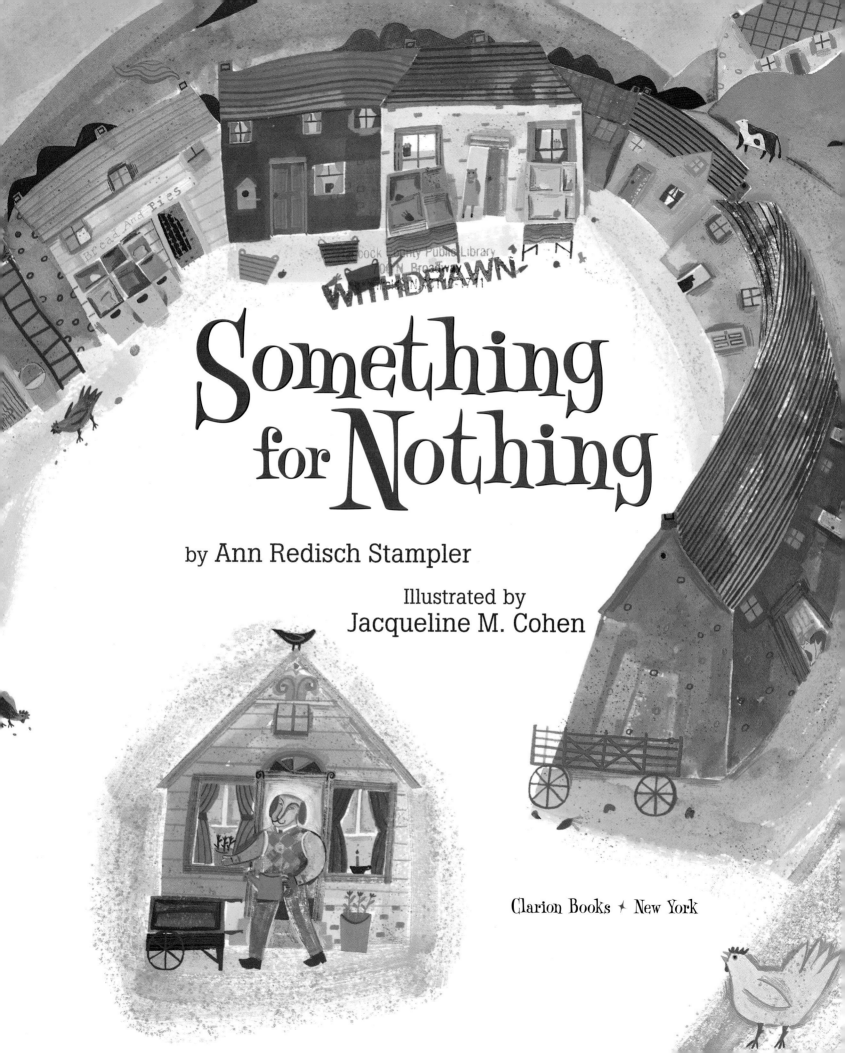

Something for Nothing

by Ann Redisch Stampler

Illustrated by
Jacqueline M. Cohen

Clarion Books ✦ New York

Right in the middle of Bialystok, there lived a big brown dog. All day long, Dog heard the hubbub of the nearby marketplace. "Potatoes! Tomatoes!" the merchants shouted. "Mackerel! Herring! Pots and pans and colanders!"

At sunset, a sweet silence fell over the neighborhood.

But as soon as the moon was high in the sky, giant wooden wagons began rumbling past. All night long, Dog heard the clip-clop of horses hauling the wagons to market. He heard the groans and shouts of workmen unloading the potatoes and tomatoes, the mackerel and herring, and the banging, clanging pans and pots and colanders, until he'd had his fill of noise.

"I will not stay in this banging, clanging, rumbling, shouting, moaning, groaning, clip-clop, clip-clop city for even one more day!" he howled.

With that, he packed all his belongings in a little red cart and set out for the countryside to search for peace and quiet. Soon, he had walked so far that when he looked back, all he could see was a little puff of smoke rising over a small hill.

For three long summer days, Dog traveled into the countryside. Then, down a crooked path, by the bank of a river, he saw an abandoned house surrounded by weeds and untended apple trees.

"This is my home!" cried Dog. He set about cleaning the house, pruning the trees, and weeding the garden. He bought tin for his roof, and he gathered stones to build a handsome path to his front door. Dog worked from sunup to sundown until his little house was all neat and bright. Then, in the blissful quiet of the country twilight, satisfied, he fell asleep.

Dog was awakened by a dreadful clatter. Terrified, he crept to the door and opened it the smallest crack. And what did he hear but howling and yowling, hissing and screeching, the sounds of branches breaking and of plants being torn from the earth!

By the light of the moon, Dog saw three big rowdy cats. They had destroyed his garden and were hurling stones and apples at his perfect country home.

"Stop it!" cried Dog.

But the rascally cats just threw more apples, laughed, and ran away.

ha Ha Ha Ha Ha Ha

EEEOOOWWW

CRRRACK

SNAPPP

CLUNK!

SPLAt

The next morning, Dog walked to the nearby inn to see what he could find out.

"Those hooligan cats are the scourge of the countryside," the innkeeper clucked. "Saturday night, they plunk their boots down on my table, slurp catnip tea, and wait for the moon to rise. Then off they go to make trouble."

Dog had not come all this way to have his country peace ruined!

"Thank you, sir," he told the innkeeper, tipping his hat. "I am just the one to teach these cats a lesson they won't soon forget."

"Oh, sir, do not fight them!" begged the innkeeper. "They will scratch you to pieces."

But Dog was gone.

In the village, Dog filled his cart with smelly old fruits and vegetables, and hauled them home. At the quarry, he filled his cart with big jagged rocks, which he hauled home and dumped at the edge of the garden.

And when Saturday came, he waited at the inn until the three rowdy cats barged through the door.

"I am so tired of country life!" Dog cried. "I miss the hubbub of Bialystok. To hear that blessed racket again, I would pay one gold zloty!"

"One gold zloty?" repeated the three cats, with a hard, greedy look in their eyes.

"But alas!" moaned Dog. "No puny country cat could possibly make enough noise."

"Why, we are the noisiest cats in all the land!" exclaimed the orange brindle cat.

"You would come to my house at moonrise, and make noise and commotion until dawn?" asked Dog.

"Of course! What could be simpler?" blustered the gray tabby cat.

"This noise would have to be loud," warned Dog. "I will not give you something for nothing."

"We will give you one gold zloty's worth of excellent commotion!" cried the spotted cat.

"You are small," sighed Dog, "but perhaps you will do." And he hurried home.

Just when the moon had risen high in the sky, the three cats marched into his garden.

"Hallooooooo!" they cried. "We are here for our gold zloty!"

"Just toss these few small things at my house," replied Dog. "And howl and yowl all the while, for if there is peace and quiet for as long as it takes to count one-two-three, I will not waste my gold zloty on you!"

"No problem!" hooted the orange brindle cat.

And the three rowdy cats began slamming and banging and throwing and screeching so loudly that the ground shook.

Dog shut his door tight, and calming himself with a bowl of warm milk, he put on his earmuffs and took refuge under the bed.

After many long hours, the banging slowed to an occasional ping and the ground ceased to shake. When Dog peered outside, he saw that the cats had fallen, exhausted, into three ragtag balls of dirty fur.

Dog leaned out the window. "Cats in Bialystok would yank potatoes from the earth and hurl them with such force, I would be scraping mashed potatoes from the walls," he declared. "But three little country cats can't even stay awake!"

"We are not sleepy!" bellowed the orange brindle cat so loudly he woke his companions. And feebly, mewing weakly, they resumed their banging and clanging.

When the first faint rays of sun shone on the still black waters of the river, Dog came into his garden with his little leather pouch, from which he drew a gleaming gold zloty. "I pay you for what others do for pleasure," he said. "But I thank you just the same."

"Then they are fools," said the orange brindle cat, snatching the zloty. "But you're welcome just the same." And the three cats limped slowly away to their beds.

Dog did not go to bed. Instead, he rushed back to the quarry, filled his cart with twice as many rocks as before, and hauled them home. He raced to the market and bought twice as many smelly old vegetables and rotten apples, which he hauled back to his garden and left sweltering in the summer sun.

The three cats had scarcely begun their morning's catnap when Dog rapped on their door, insisting that they come back to his cottage to make more noise and commotion.

"Noooooo!" moaned the orange brindle cat from his bed. "Our paws are sore from throwing, and our voices hoarse from screeching!"

"Pleeeeease," coaxed Dog. "For just a little more racket, I would pay *two* gold zlotys, for I won't give you something for nothing."

"Two gold zlotys!" squealed the three cats.

At moonrise, the three rowdy cats arrived at Dog's cottage, where they hurled twice as many rocks and vegetables, made twice as much terrible racket, and stumbled home twice as tired as before.

But Dog was not finished. As soon as the cats had limped away, he rushed back to the quarry for more giant rocks and to the market for more smelly old vegetables and apples.

"Go away!" groaned the three cats when Dog rapped on their door. "Let us sleep!"

"Three gold zlotys . . ." murmured Dog. "For just a little more racket, I'll pay *three* gold zlotys. But I want my noise, for I won't give you something for nothing."

"Three gold zlotys!" cried the three greedy cats.

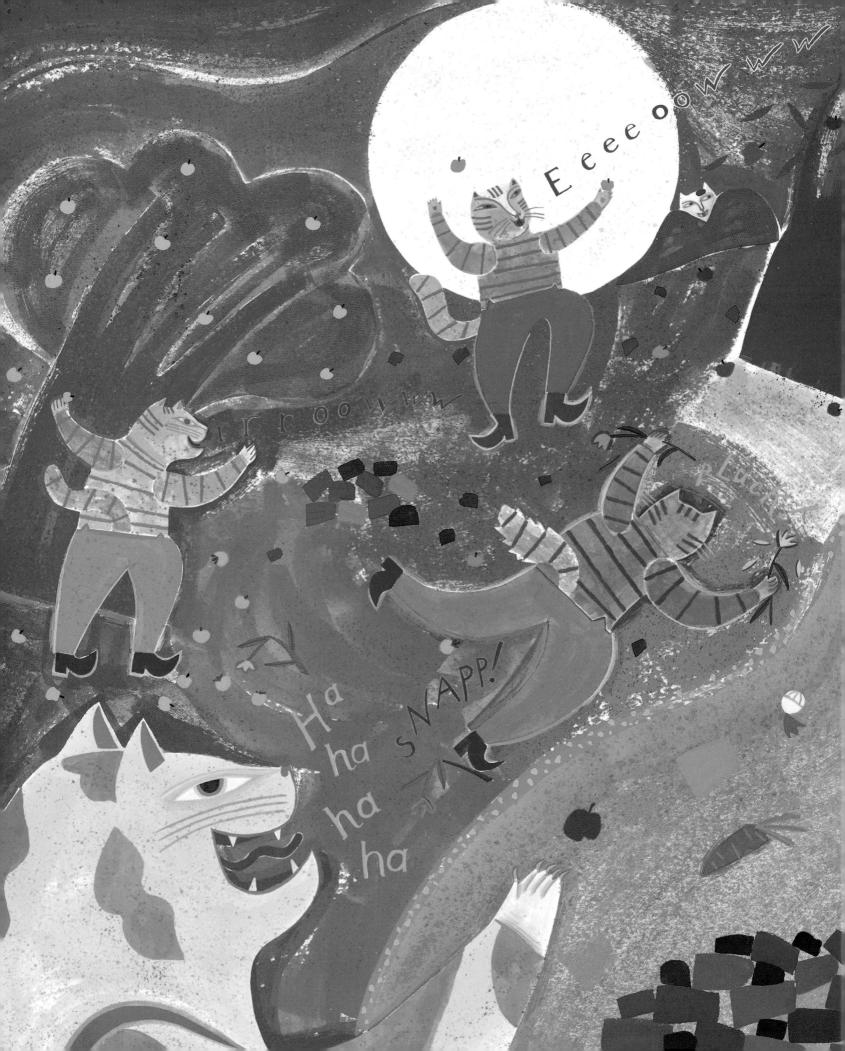

At moonrise, the cats dragged themselves to Dog's cottage, where they threw three times as many rocks and three times as many rotten apples and old vegetables, made three times as much racket . . .

25

. . . and crawled home three times more exhausted than before.

For the rest of the week, Dog scraped and pruned and hammered
from sunup to sundown. When Saturday came, he rested until
the afternoon shadows grew long.

Then he picked himself up and trudged back to the inn, where he found the three rowdy cats.

"Hallo, Dog!" cried the orange brindle cat, guzzling a bucket of catnip tea. "Have ever you seen such a feast? We have been eating all day long on your gold zlotys!"

"I have come to thank you for the noise and commotion," said Dog. "You did your best for three nights, and it was almost good enough."

"Almost!" screeched the cats. "Why, we worked every moment for three long nights for those gold zlotys! Why, when we went home at daybreak, we were all sore and bent over."

Dog sighed. "The cats in Bialystok cavort all night and dance the next day, too," he said. "I wish you little country cats would try again."

The orange brindle cat looked Dog hard in the eye.

"There is no city beast that makes more noise than we do," he declared. "Besides, my comrades are not eager to help you again, so it would cost you a little bit more."

"How I yearn for you to scream and stomp and bang all night!" moaned Dog. "But alas, I cannot pay you, for those were my only zlotys, and there are no more."

"No more?" bellowed the orange brindle cat.

"No more," sighed Dog, hiding a little smile behind his paw. "But would you possibly consider coming back to bang and clang and tear the apples from the trees all night, just for the pleasure of it?"

The cats jumped up from the table. "What do you take us for? Three country fools?" shouted the gray tabby cat.

"You want us to scream and stomp and bang all night until our backs hurt and our heads ache and our paws are numb—for nothing?" howled the spotted cat.

"We want our gold zlotys!" cried the orange brindle cat. "If you want us to bother you, you must pay, for we will not give you something for nothing!"

And with that, the three rowdy cats stomped out of the inn, and true to their word, they never disturbed the peace and quiet of Dog's country cottage ever again.

Author's Note

Something for Nothing fits squarely into the genre of Yiddish tales in which a clever protagonist outsmarts evildoers. The story as I first heard it was a cautionary tale that conveyed not only the protagonist's cleverness but also the perils of life in Europe when my grandmother was young. The characters were people, not animals—a little Jewish tailor and a gang of bloodthirsty villagers—and the hero avoided not just mischief but a massacre.

My grandmother told me the story as we were sitting in her garden shelling peas. She had come to the United States from Poland just before World War I, settled in northern Vermont, worked hard, and eventually purchased a small hotel in New Hampshire. By the time I was born, the family, friends, and villages she had known in Poland had been destroyed in World War II; we children were discouraged from asking about the terrible losses, from speaking Yiddish, and from romanticizing the culture.

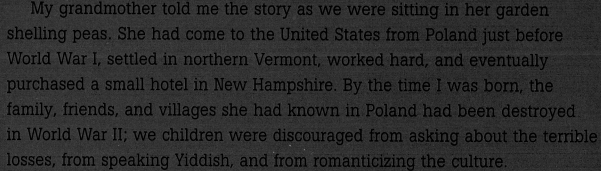

The particulars of my grandmother's years in Poland are obscure, but this story tells us something about the life she left behind. The frightening reality that Jews in the countryside of Eastern Europe could not expect a safe and peaceful life is transformed here into a joke in which the underdog prevails. This use of humor is typical of the way my grandmother and others in her culture came to cope with the tribulations of their daily lives.

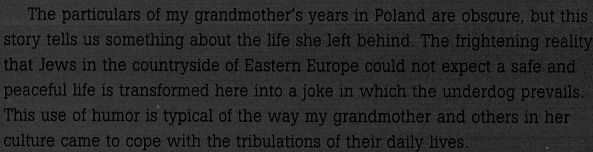

As I was attempting to trace the roots of this story, my mother-in-law, who was born in Poland and raised in the Urals, and a dear friend who lived near Bialystok both said the story sounded familiar. However, despite the generous assistance of Dr. Dan Ben-Amos at the University of Pennsylvania, no written record of it has been located.

The spirit of our tales and of our storytellers remains with us. Thirty years after that afternoon in my grandmother's garden, I heard my mother telling her version of the story to my children. I decided to write it down in a form that I hope children can enjoy today. I am honored to be the one to preserve this wry bit of our history.